Yaffa and Fatima

Author's Note

This story was inspired by a tale that is said to have both Jewish and Arab origins. Florence Freedman (*Brothers A Hebrew Legend*), Elaine Lindy (*Two Brothers*), Amy Friedman and Meredith Johnson (*The Two Brothers*) all capture the beauty of the story's message. Although the traditional tale is about two brothers, my version is about two neighbors—one Jewish and one Muslim—incorporating the message of appreciating people for who they are.
– F.G.-W.

To my nephew Gabriel DiFilippo who makes the world a better place. I love you. –F.G.-W.

To Gabriella and Dina for their support –C.F.

Text copyright © 2017 by Fawzia Gilani-Williams
Illustrations copyright © 2017 by Lerner Publishing Group, Inc.

KAR-BEN PUBLISHING
A division of Lerner Publishing Group, Inc.
241 First Avenue North
Minneapolis, MN 55401 USA
1-800-4-Karben

Website address: www.karben.com

Main body text set in Adrianna Demibold. Typeface provided by Chank.

Library of Congress Cataloging-in-Publication Data

Names: Gilani-Williams, Fawzia, author. | Fedele, Chiara, illustrator.
Title: Yaffa and Fatima : shalom, salaam / by Fawzia Gilani-Williams ; illustrated by Chiara Fedele.
Description: Minneapolis : Kar-Ben Publishing, [2017] | Summary: "Yaffa and Fatima live on neighboring date farms. When very little rain leads to a poor harvest, both women go to extra measures to make sure that their neighbor doesn't go hungry"— Provided by publisher.
Identifiers: LCCN 2016009545 (print) | LCCN 2016029273 (ebook) | ISBN 9781467789387 (lb : alk. paper) | ISBN 9781467794237 (pb : alk. paper) | ISBN 9781512427172 (eb pdf)
Subjects: | CYAC: Friendship—Fiction. | Muslims—Fiction. | Jews—Israel—Fiction. | Israel—Fiction.
Classification: LCC PZ7.G372 Yaf 2017 (print) | LCC PZ7.G372 (ebook) | DDC [E]—dc23

LC record available at https://lccn.loc.gov/2016009545

PJ Library Edition ISBN 978-1-5124-6071-1

Manufactured in China
1-43047-27707-10/2/2020

042128.5K2/B1038/A5

Yaffa and Fatima
Shalom, Salaam

adapted by Fawzia Gilani-Williams
illustrations by Chiara Fedele

KAR-BEN
PUBLISHING

In a beautiful land, called the Land of Milk and Honey, there lived two neighbors. One was named *Yaffa* and the other was named *Fatima*.

Yaffa and Fatima each owned a beautiful date grove. During the week they both worked very hard gathering their dates.

On most days Yaffa and Fatima sold all their dates at the market and were able to buy plenty of tasty food to eat—which they often shared.

Yaffa loved Fatima's shwarma. And Fatima loved Yaffa's schnitzel.

Yaffa prayed in the synagogue.

Fatima prayed in the mosque.

They both loved God, and they both loved to follow God's way.

Yaffa would read from her Siddur in the morning.

Fatima would read from her Qur'an in the morning.

Yaffa fasted on Yom Kippur.

Fatima fasted during Ramadan.

Fatima celebrated Eid.

Yaffa celebrated Passover.

When Yaffa saw Fatima,
she would wave and call,
"Shalom! Peace!"

When Fatima saw Yaffa,
she would wave and call,
"Salaam! Peace!"

One year there was very little rain.
Fatima and Yaffa had very few dates
to eat or to sell at the market.

Yaffa lay awake at night. She was worried.

"Maybe Fatima is hungry," thought Yaffa.

Fatima lay awake at night.
She was worried.

"Perhaps Yaffa didn't
have enough to eat
today," thought Fatima.

Fatima placed a basket of dates on her donkey. Then she took them to Yaffa's house. She poured the dates into a basket on Yaffa's porch.

Meanwhile, Yaffa collected a basket of dates, placed it on her donkey, and carried it to Fatima's house. She poured the dates into a basket on Fatima's porch.

The two neighbors quietly made their
way back home feeling happy.

In the morning when Yaffa walked onto her porch, to her great surprise, she saw her basket full of dates.

"Goodness! I have so many dates! I will take more to Fatima tonight."

Meanwhile, Fatima walked out onto her porch and was just as surprised.

"Goodness! I have more dates than I thought! I will take some more to Yaffa tonight."

That night both Yaffa and Fatima loaded their donkeys with dates and set off toward each other's homes.

They met just where their fields came together.

Fatima looked at Yaffa. Yaffa looked at Fatima.

The two friends hugged each other and laughed.

"*Shalom*," said Yaffa.

"*Salaam*," said Fatima.

"Thank you for thinking of me," said Yaffa.

"Thank you for thinking of me too," said Fatima.

Together, they returned to Yaffa's house to share a meal of dates and tea.